Diego and the Magic Box

Shawn Gregoire
and
Diego Gregoire

To order additional copies of this book, contact:
Xlibris
1-888-795-4274
www.Xlibris.com
Orders@Xlibris.com

ISBN: Softcover 978-1-9845-7803-7
Hardcover 978-1-9845-7804-4
EBook 978-1-9845-7802-0

Print information available on the last page

Rev. date: 05/08/2020

Diego and the Magic Box

I'm so bored. I have all these old toys, and I don't want to play with them.

It's raining outside, so Mom and Dad
don't want to take me anywhere to play.

What do I do? Maybe I'll
just be bored forever.

I’m sad.

Hmm, I've never seen this box before . . .

Wow, I fit in the box too.
What if I just make believe?

Maybe this box can turn into a boat . . .
I can sail across the seas and be a pirate!

Or maybe this box can be a
really fast airplane . . .
I can fly through the air and
make circles through the clouds!

What if the box was a rocket?

I could count down
5...4...3...2...1
and lift off all the
way into outer
space.

What if the box . . .
could make me disappear?

I could close the box and then

poof, nobody would be able to find me.

"Diego! Everything okay, buddy? Where are you?

“Wow, I can’t find him anywhere.

"Hellooooo, has anyone seen Diego?"
HEE - HEE

"Here I am, Dad!"

"Whoa! Where did you go?"
"I was in this box the whole time!
It's magic!"

Maybe I don't need new toys or to go outside to have fun after all.

Sometimes, all I need is my imagination and I can be anything I want . . .

But it also helps to have a *magic box*.

Lightning Source UK Ltd.
Milton Keynes UK
UKHW050625010620
364137UK00002B/70